# LITTLE GREEN FINGERS

Written by
Clare Chandler

Illustrated by
Helen Holroyd

Designed by
Wayne Blades

Edited by
Kay Barnham and Hazel Songhurst

Whitecap Books Ltd.
Vancouver/Toronto

**Clare Chandler** is an experienced children's writer and gardener.

Produced by **Zigzag Publishing Ltd**,
The Barn, Randolph's Farm, Brighton Road,
Hurstpierpoint, Sussex, BN6 9EL, England

Illustrator: Helen Holroyd
Designer: Wayne Blades
Editor: Kay Barnham
Editorial Manager: Hazel Songhurst
Director of Editorial: Jen Green
Production: Zoë Fawcett and Simon Eaton
Concept: Tony Potter, Hazel Songhurst, Wayne Blades

Colour separations: Singapore
Printed in Singapore

This edition published by
Whitecap Books Ltd,
351 Lynn Avenue, North Vancouver,
British Columbia VJ7 2C4

Copyright © 1996 Zigzag Publishing Ltd.

ISBN 1 55110 258 7

# CONTENTS

# ABOUT THIS BOOK

Gardening is great fun. It is very exciting to see your plants grow and the tiny seeds you plant become beautiful flowers. This book will show you all the skills you need to become a good gardener. Learn how to sow seeds, take cuttings and care for your plants.

There are things to grow in pots if you do not have your own patch of ground. There are bulbs to grow to brighten up the winter months, window boxes and a wild west garden to make.

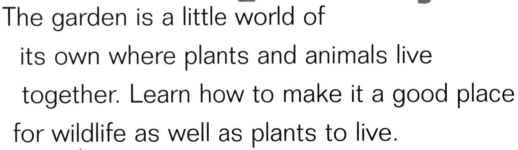

You can grow delicious vegetables and tasty herbs to eat with them.

The garden is a little world of its own where plants and animals live together. Learn how to make it a good place for wildlife as well as plants to live.

# HOW PLANTS GROW

Plants need light, water and warmth to grow. They get warmth and light from the sun. Their roots suck up water and tiny food particles from the soil.

A good gardener makes sure his or her plants have everything they need.

Shoots grow up from seeds or bulbs and push through the soil.

Roots grow down into the soil.

The shoots grow into plants.

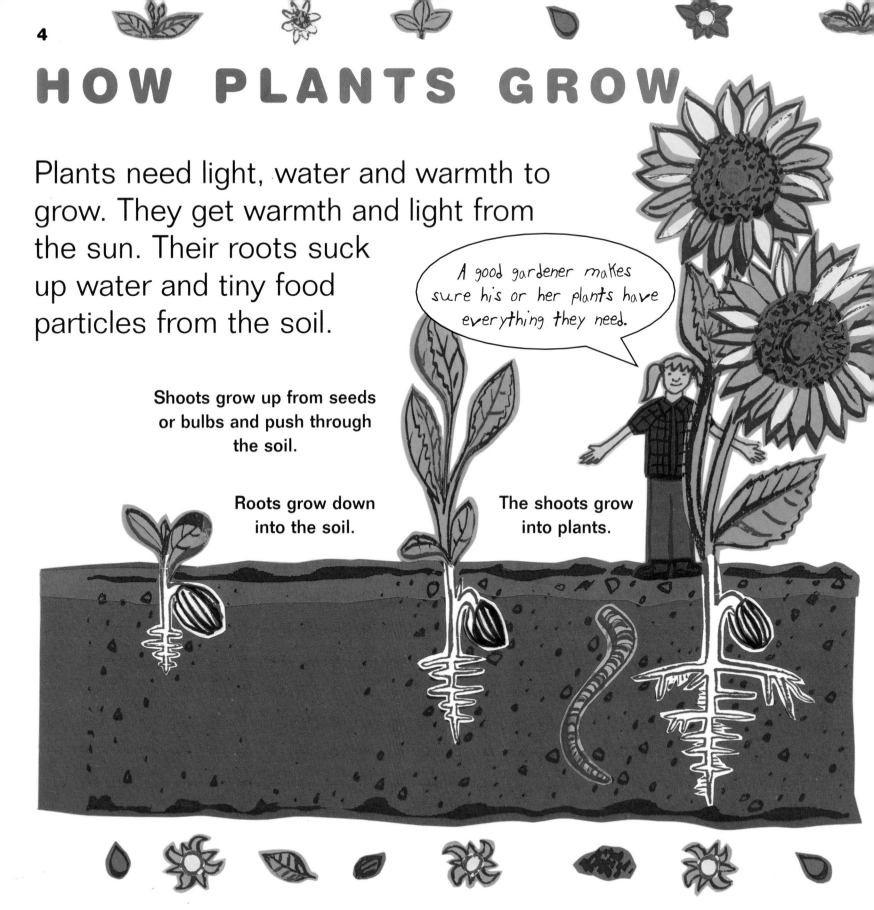

# Looking After Plants

Grow plants where they can get plenty of light.

A plant in a pot needs potting soil. Garden soil does not contain all the food it needs to grow.

Push your finger into the soil as deep as your fingernail. If it feels dry, the plant needs water.

Water plants regularly, but do not overwater or they may die.

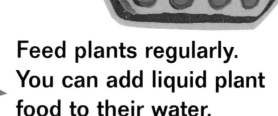

Feed plants regularly. You can add liquid plant food to their water.

Give plants more to drink when it is hot.

## TRY THIS

Watch beans make roots and shoots! Roll up a piece of blotting paper and put it in a jam jar. Push a few broad beans between the paper and the glass and put a little water in the bottom.

In a few weeks, the shoots will appear.

In about 10 days the roots begin to grow.

Make sure the paper stays damp.

# GROWING FROM SEEDS

## YOU WILL NEED

seeds

rake

fork

watering can

flower pots

patch of ground

If you sow seeds outdoors in spring, you will have a garden full of flowers in the summer. Flowers also grow happily in tubs and pots of all different shapes and sizes.

**Wait until the weather is getting warm. When the grass on the lawn starts to grow, the soil is warm enough for sowing seeds in the garden.**

**1. Dig over the ground with a fork. Rake the soil smooth, taking out any large lumps of earth or stones.**

**2. Sprinkle the seeds evenly over the ground. Rake again.**

## TRY THIS

**Carefully cut the stem of a white carnation in half, from the bottom to the top. Put one half of the stem in a cup of red food colouring. Put the other half in a cup of blue food colouring. Leave overnight and see what happens!**

# Flowers To Grow

nasturtium

cornflower

marigold

candytuft

virginia stock

nigella

california poppy

Remember to read the instructions on seed packets. They will tell you where and when to plant seeds and how tall the flowers will grow.

3. Water very lightly, sprinkling from a watering can.

4. In two or three months, you should have fully grown plants.

# A WINDOW BOX

## YOU WILL NEED

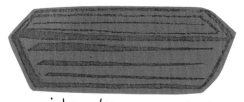

window box    small plants

bulbs    stones

potting soil

trowel

watering can    plant food

Plant a box full of flowers on a window ledge. It will brighten up your home all year round. Choose small plants and some that will trail over the sides.

Ask a grown-up to fix the box securely on the window ledge. If it slopes, wedge pieces of wood under the front of the box to keep it level.

Put some stones in the bottom of the box. Half fill it with potting soil. Take your plants out of their pots, put them in the box and firmly press more soil around the roots.

# Spring

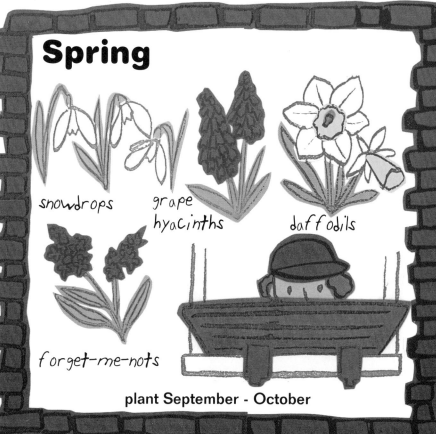

snowdrops

grape hyacinths

daffodils

forget-me-nots

plant September - October

# Summer

daisies

impatiens

marigolds

petunias

plant May

# Autumn

lobelia (trailing)

geraniums

plant June - July

# Winter

winter pansies

ivy (small variegated)

Add plant food to the water once a month.

plant September in warmer regions

# TAKING CUTTINGS

| YOU WILL NEED |
|---|

A cutting is part of a plant that you cut off to make another plant. If you take cuttings in the spring, you will soon have lots of new plants. Geraniums, fuchsias, pinks, impatiens and mint all grow well from cuttings.

a plant

trowel

jar of water

sharp scissors

potting soil

pot

Only take cuttings from strong, healthy plants. Choose a stem that has leaves on it but no flowers. Use sharp scissors to cut off the stem.

# Flowers To Grow

1. Pull off the leaves from the base of the cutting.

2. Put the cutting in a jar of water.

geranium

pink

fuchsia

mint

impatiens

3. Wait for it to grow roots.

4. When the roots have grown, take the cutting out of the water and plant it in a pot full of damp potting soil.

# INDOOR BULBS

**YOU WILL NEED**

Grow spring flowers in the winter by planting bulbs indoors. Start in the early autumn for flowers in January or February. Hyacinths and daffodils are the easiest to grow, but you could try crocuses and tulips too.

bulbs

shallow pot

**1. Half fill the pot with bulb fibre or potting soil. Put in the bulbs, making sure the pointed ends face upwards.**

**2. Pack the soil around the bulbs, but do not cover them completely. Now leave the pot in a cool, dark place.**

small trowel

bulb fibre
or potting soil

top

bottom

A garden shed or a garage is an ideal place to keep your bulbs.

3. In a few weeks, you will see shoots growing. Bring the pot into the light but keep it away from direct heat.

## TRY THIS

Grow a hyacinth in water! It is fascinating to see the long roots grow down from the bulb. Use a special hyacinth jar. Fill it with clean water to about 1 cm from the top. Put the jar in a cool, dark place until the shoots appear, then bring it in to the light.

4. When the shoots are about 6 cm tall, put the pot on a windowsill. Watch for the flowers to appear.

# WILDLIFE GARDEN

Make a corner of your garden into a wildlife sanctuary. It will attract all kinds of birds, minibeasts and other animals.

wildflower seeds

rake

Start in autumn or spring. Dig over and rake a patch of ground. Scatter the wildflower seeds over the soil and water well. Do not sow them in rows – your wildlife garden should not look too neat.

water

patch of ground

## TRY THIS

**Make a bug jar that helps you collect minibeasts without harming them. Push two lengths of plastic tubing through the top. Put the end of one tube over the minibeast and suck in through the other tube. The air will pull the minibeast gently into the jar.**

Look carefully at the minibeasts, then let them go.

long tube

short tube

suck gently on this end

Ask a grown-up to help you make a bird table. Put out water and food for the birds. They like seeds, nuts, apple or coconut. Do not forget to fill your table during the winter.

# SUNFLOWERS

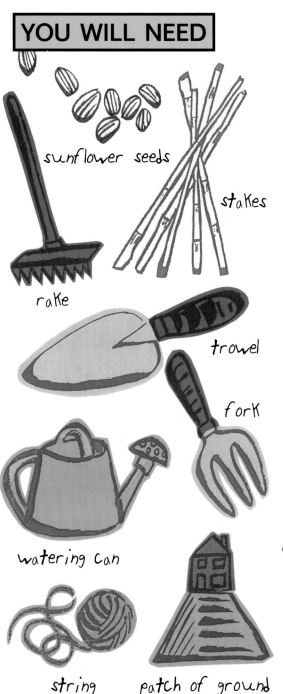

YOU WILL NEED

sunflower seeds

stakes

rake

trowel

fork

watering can

string

patch of ground

Sunflowers get their name from their huge golden flowers. They grow very quickly. Plant seeds with your friends and see whose grows tallest.

Leave about 50 cm between each seed.

Keep watering and they will grow quickly.

In the spring, plant the seeds in a sunny place. Push each seed into the soil until your fingernail is covered. Water the ground every day. The shoots will appear in the next two weeks.

When the sunflowers have reached a height of about 60 cm, push stakes firmly into the ground next to them. Tie the stems to the stakes to support them.

**TRY THIS**
In the autumn, collect seeds from lots of different flowers. Put them in separate envelopes and draw the flowers on the front so you will recognize them next spring.

Watch the sunflowers' heads turn during the day to face the sun.

# HERB GARDEN

YOU WILL NEED

seeds

pots

potting soil

string    labels    jars

watering can

Herbs are easy to grow. They have pretty leaves and many have flowers too. Herbs smell lovely and you can use them for flavouring your food.

**In spring you can grow herbs from seeds. Fill a pot with soil. Water it and scatter a few seeds on top. Press them in gently.**

**Label the pots.**

**Mint and rosemary grow well from cuttings (see pages 6 and 7). Parsley and tarragon should be bought as plants.**

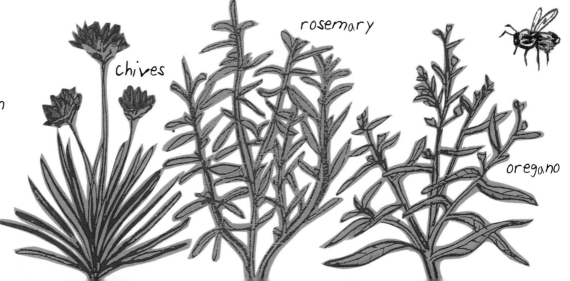
chives    rosemary    oregano

Chop some parsley and mint or chives. Crush a clove of garlic. Mix them all into cream cheese. Spread it on bread for a delicious snack.

1. Dry your herbs in the summer and you will be able to cook with them during the winter. Pick them on a dry day before they flower. Hang bundles of herbs in a dry place.

2. Two weeks later take them down. Rub the leaves off the stems with your fingers and put them in labelled jars.

Cut growing shoots to make the plant grow bushier. Use these herb shoots in recipes.

thyme

mint

parsley

# POT OF POTATOES

Grow a whole pot of potatoes from one old sprouting potato!

sprouting potato

very large pot

stones

potting soil

watering can

1. Find a potato that has sprouted shoots. Leave two strong shoots and rub off the rest with your thumb. Put stones in the bottom of a very large pot. Half fill it with soil and put the potato in with the shoots facing up.

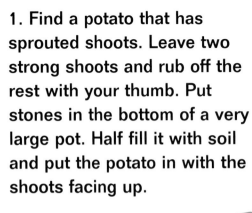

2. Cover with soil and water. As they grow, cover the shoots with soil until the pot is full.

## TRY THIS

Make a potato maze to show how plants grow towards light. Make a hole in the short side of a shoe box. Stick some pieces of cardboard inside the box to make a maze. Put a sprouting potato at the opposite end to the hole. Put on the lid. After a few days, look and see if the shoot is finding its way out.

3. Water it regularly and in a couple of months you will have a large plant with small white flowers. Stop watering when the flowers die.

4. When the whole plant dies it is time to harvest your crop. Carefully tip the pot out on to newspaper and see how many potatoes you have grown.

# PESTS AND FRIENDS

**YOU WILL NEED**

old plastic bowl

spade

patch of ground

pond weed

large stones

Some of the animals that live in the garden are pests. For example, slugs and aphids eat our plants. However, gardeners do have many animal friends. Bees pollinate our flowers, worms turn dead leaves into fertilizer, and others, like toads and birds, help by eating the pests.

**Friends**

birds

worms

dragonflies

ladybugs

bees

toads

frogs

slugs

aphids

caterpillars

snails

**Pests**

# TRY THIS

**Grow marigolds (see pages 8 and 9) because they attract dragonflies, which eat lots of aphids. If you still have aphids, spray them with soapy water and rub them off the plant gently with your fingers.**

Do not use poison to kill pests because it will also get rid of some of your garden friends.

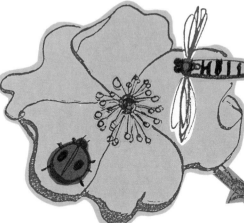

Keep your plants well-fed and watered because pests will attack mainly the weak, unhealthy ones.

A pond will encourage many friends, including birds, frogs and toads. A toad's favourite snack is a juicy slug! Make a pond by sinking a plastic bowl into the ground. Fill it with water and add pond weed and large stones.

# TASTY TOMATOES

tomato plants

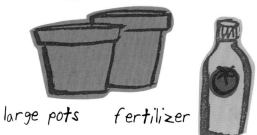
large pots     fertilizer

potting soil

watering can     string

stakes

Freshly-picked home-grown tomatoes are delicious – much tastier than the ones you buy. Buy small tomato plants in the spring.

**1.** Fill a big pot with potting soil. Push a stake firmly into it and make another hole for the plant.

**2.** Tip the plant out of its pot and put it in the hole. Cover the roots with soil and pat it down. Water the soil well.

3. Put the pot in a warm, sunny place. Water the soil every day. Add fertilizer to the water once a week. Tie the plant to the stake as it grows.

4. Look out for tiny side shoots that grow where the large leaf stalks join the main stem. Pinch these off to stop your plant growing too bushy.

5. Pick the tomatoes when they are bright red.

Make tomato chutney using red or green tomatoes. Ask an adult to help you cook it, as the mixture can become very hot!

# WILD WEST GARDEN

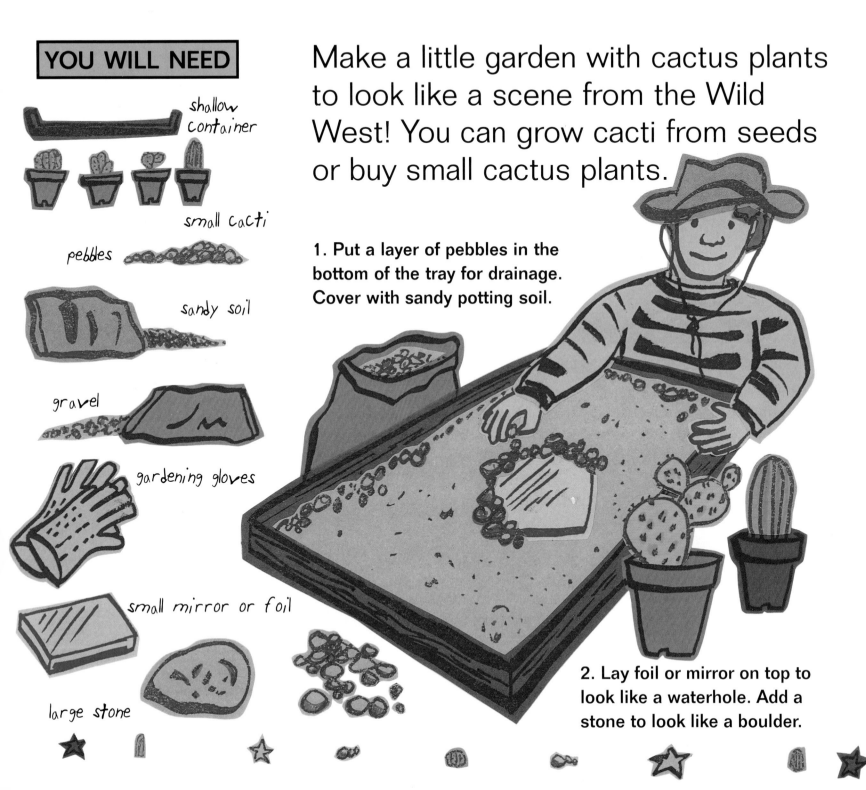

**YOU WILL NEED**

shallow container

small cacti

pebbles

sandy soil

gravel

gardening gloves

small mirror or foil

large stone

Make a little garden with cactus plants to look like a scene from the Wild West! You can grow cacti from seeds or buy small cactus plants.

1. Put a layer of pebbles in the bottom of the tray for drainage. Cover with sandy potting soil.

2. Lay foil or mirror on top to look like a waterhole. Add a stone to look like a boulder.

3. Make a hole in the soil to plant each cactus. Wear thick gardening gloves to protect your fingers from the spines.

4. Water the soil lightly. Put a layer of gravel over the soil. Add a few toy horses and cowboys or cowgirls.

Cacti are desert plants, so they like to be in a warm place without much water. In winter let the soil almost dry out. If you look after them they may surprise you with brightly coloured flowers.

# GARDEN PRESENTS

Many of the things you grow will make good gifts. Take care to make them look special.

Put spare cuttings or seedlings in decorated pots.

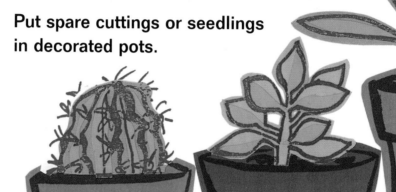

Make little bags for your dried herbs and tie them with ribbon. Fill a small basket or box with tomatoes or potatoes.

Write a friend's name or initials in cress. Cut out the letters from paper towel and dampen with water. Scatter the seeds over the letters. Keep them damp until they have grown.